Princess Ponies
A Magical Friend

P9-CAB-615

The Princess Ponies series

Princess Ponies

A Magical Friend

CHLOE RYDER

BLOOMSBURY

NEW YORK LONDON OXFORD NEW DELHI SYDNEY

Text copyright © 2013 by Awesome Media and Entertainment Ltd
Illustrations copyright © 2013 by Jennifer Miles
All rights reserved. No part of this book may be reproduced or transmitted in any form
or by any means, electronic or mechanical, including photocopying, recording, or by any
information storage and retrieval system, without permission in writing from the publisher.

First published in Great Britain in March 2013 by Bloomsbury Publishing Plc
Published in the United States of America in March 2014
by Bloomsbury Children's Books
www.bloomsbury.com

For information about permission to reproduce selections from this book, write to
Permissions, Bloomsbury Children's Books, 1385 Broadway, New York, New York 10018
Bloomsbury books may be purchased for business or promotional use. For information on
bulk purchases please contact Macmillan Corporate and Premium Sales Department at
specialmarkets@macmillan.com

Library of Congress Cataloging-in-Publication Data
Ryder, Chloe.
A magical friend / Chloe Ryder.
pages   cm. — (Princess ponies ; 1)
Summary: On an enchanted island, far, far away, princess ponies can talk and
play. Eight golden horseshoes give the ponies their magic, but when the shoes go
missing from the castle, only a true pony lover can save the princesses and their
home. Can Pippa and Stardust work together to find the golden horseshoes?
ISBN 978-1-61963-165-6 (paperback) • ISBN 978-1-61963-166-3 (e-book)
[1. Ponies—Fiction. 2. Magic—Fiction. 3. Princesses—Fiction.
4. Friendship—Fiction.] I. Title.
PZ7.R95898Mag 2014   [Fic]—dc23   2013034318

Typeset by Hewer Text UK Ltd, Edinburgh
Printed in China by Leo Paper Products, Heshan, Guangdong
6 8 10 9 7

All papers used by Bloomsbury Publishing, Inc., are natural, recyclable products
made from wood grown in well-managed forests. The manufacturing processes
conform to the environmental regulations of the country of origin.

With special thanks to Julie Sykes

The Pony

Queen
Moonshine

Princess
Crystal

Princess
Cloud

Princess
Stardust

Princess
Honey

Royal Family

King
Firestar

Prince
Jet

Prince
Comet

Prince
Storm

Early one morning, just before dawn, two ponies stood in an ancient court-yard, looking sadly at a stone wall.

"In all my life this wall has never been empty. I can't believe that the horse-shoes have been taken—and just before Midsummer Day too," said the stallion.

He was a handsome animal—a copper-colored pony, with strong legs and bright eyes, dressed in a royal red sash.

1

The mare was a dainty yet majestic palomino with a golden coat and a pure white tail that fell to the ground like a waterfall.

She whinnied softly. "We don't have much time to find them all."

With growing sadness the two ponies watched the night fade away and the sun rise. When the first ray of sunlight spread into the courtyard it lit up the wall, showing the imprints where the golden horseshoes should have been hanging.

"Midsummer Day is the longest day of the year," said the stallion quietly. "It's the time when our ancient horseshoes must renew their magical energy. If the horseshoes are still missing in eight days, then by nightfall on the

3

eighth day, their magic will fade and our beautiful island will be no more."

Sighing heavily, he touched his nose to his queen's.

"Only a miracle can save us now," he said.

The queen dipped her head, the diamonds on her crown sparkling in the early morning light.

"Have faith," she said gently. "I sense that a miracle is coming."

Chapter 1

Pippa MacDonald turned her pony, Snowdrop, toward the last jump, a solid-looking red-and-white wall. Snowdrop pricked up her ears. She snorted with excitement and sped up.

"Steady, girl," Pippa said, pulling gently on the reins.

None of the other riders had jumped a clean round. Pippa and Snowdrop were the last to go, and if they cleared the wall they would win the competition, taking home a silver cup and a blue ribbon. As the wall came closer, Pippa forced back the nervous, fluttery feeling growing in her stomach.

"We can do this," she whispered to Snowdrop.

She leaned forward, standing up in her stirrups, loosening the reins as she pushed her pony to the jump. Snowdrop leaped over it eagerly, carrying Pippa upward. For a magical moment it felt like they were flying. Any fear of heights simply slipped away. Fresh air rushed at Pippa's face, lifting her dark, wavy hair that was neatly held in place by a hairnet. Snowdrop cleared the wall, happily flicking her tail as she landed.

"Yes!" Pippa shouted, galloping Snowdrop over the finish line.

The crowd cheered and screamed, but one voice shouted louder than the rest.

"Pippa! Are you awake? It's time to go."

Pippa jolted out of her dream, nearly falling off her bed as Snowdrop, the show jumping arena, and the cheering crowds vanished. She blinked and stared around the small bedroom she shared with her big sister, Miranda.

It was easy to see which side of the room was Pippa's. Her wall was totally covered with pictures of ponies—big ones, small ones, black, brown, chestnut, roan, palomino, gray. Pippa's favorite picture of all was of Snowdrop, a silver-colored pony with deep-brown eyes.

Miranda's side used to have horse pictures too, but it was now covered with posters of boys—some were famous movie stars but most were in bands. Both sisters thought the other one's decorations were silly.

"Are you ready, sweetheart?" Mom asked from the doorway.

"Almost!" Pippa called, jumping off the bed and following her mom downstairs. "Did you remember to pack my bathing suit?"

"Of course," Mom said, smiling. "Now go get ready!"

☆

It was boiling hot and Pippa was glad that she, her mom, Miranda, and their little brother, Jack, were going on vacation, trading their apartment in the city for a cottage by the sea. Pippa was so excited she trotted up and down the pavement, riding an imaginary pony as she waited for Mom to unlock the car so that they could load the luggage into the trunk.

"You're so immature," Miranda said, rolling her eyes as she climbed into the front seat.

Mom snapped Jack into his car seat and Pippa took her usual seat in the back, beside her brother.

"We're off!" cheered Pippa as Mom started the engine.

Dreamily, Pippa stared out the window, watching the busy city streets change to green fields filled with horses, cows, and sheep, until at last they arrived at their vacation home.

"Wow! Is it all ours?" Pippa exclaimed, as Mom pulled up in front of a small, white cottage surrounded by a huge yard. "I could have a pony if we lived here."

"Yes, the yard's big enough!" Mom

agreed, digging in her handbag for the key to the front door.

The cottage was right by the water. Pippa breathed deeply, loving the smell of the fresh, salty air.

"Can we go to the beach?" she asked.

Mom laughed at her impatience. "Let's unpack the car first. If we're going to the beach, you'll want to take your buckets and shovels."

"I'll help," Pippa said, pulling her bag from the trunk.

The cottage was even prettier inside. Pippa loved the attic bedroom, even though she had to share it with Miranda. It had sloping walls and a sea view, and, to Pippa's delight, there was an old horseshoe nailed to one of the roof beams.

"Horseshoes are lucky," she said happily.

Pippa skipped down the stairs into the kitchen, where Mom was searching their luggage for the bag of food.

"We'll have our lunch on the beach," she said, packing sandwiches, cupcakes, apples, and drinks into a picnic basket.

☆

The gate at the back of the yard opened onto a winding path that led down to the sea. Pippa was too excited to walk. Instead she galloped down the path, pretending to be a wild stallion, until she reached a horseshoe-shaped cove. Pippa stared in wonder at the golden sand and sparkling blue water stretching away from her.

The cove felt so secret and special it made Pippa's insides buzz with excitement.

"It's magic," she whispered softly.

Pulling off her sandals, she ran across the powdery sand to the sea, where tiny, white-crested waves were licking the shore. Just as Pippa was about to paddle in the water, she saw something far away. What was that at the mouth of the cove?

Pippa stared in amazement at two animals splashing in the water. "They look just like seahorses!" she gasped.

Pippa raised her arm to shield her eyes from the sun so she could take a better look. They really did look like seahorses, and they were almost as big as real horses, with gracefully curved necks bobbing above the water and long spines sticking up along spiky manes. One horse was pale pink and the other was green with dark freckles. Pippa blinked and rubbed her eyes. Was she imagining things? When she looked again the two animals were still there, splashing water at each other with their curled tails.

Behind her Pippa could hear Mom, Miranda, and Jack laughing together as they made their way to the beach.

"Quick!" she called, waving at them. "Look at this!"

"What is it, sweetheart?"

"Seahorses," Pippa said.

"Where? I can't see them!" Jack cried.

"Seahorses!" Miranda exclaimed.

"How can you see a tiny seahorse from here?"

"They're giant ones," Pippa said.

"I can't see anything." Mom stared out at the sea.

Miranda giggled as she ran over. "I see them! The red one's wearing a hat!"

Pippa's heart leaped, then sank right down to her bare toes. Miranda was teasing her! Besides, the sea was empty now. The seahorses had disappeared.

"I did see two seahorses," Pippa insisted. "They were playing together."

"Don't be silly, Pip. There's no such thing as a giant seahorse," Miranda said meanly.

"Pippa, you're too big for that sort of

make-believe," Mom said gently. "Come and help me set out the picnic."

Pippa gazed at the sea, but there was nothing there except for the sea-gulls gliding over the bay. But the seahorses *were* real—Pippa knew she hadn't imagined them. Confused, she hurried after Mom.

"Do I have to eat now?" she asked. "I want to go in the water first."

"Go ahead," Mom said. "Be careful. Don't go in deeper than your knees."

Pippa ran back to the water's edge. The sea was lovely and warm. She waded out until she was knee deep. The water was so clear she could still see her feet. Pippa wiggled her toes in the sand.

"Ooooh," she said. "That tickles!"

Two tiny seahorses were swimming around her feet.

"Wow! This place is full of seahorses!" Pippa bent down for a closer look.

The moment her fingers touched the water they began to tingle. The feeling was so incredible that Pippa felt sure it was some kind of magic. Gently, she moved her fingers to get one of the seahorses to swim to her hand. The tiny animal was almost there when, suddenly, with a loud *whoosh*, the water rose up in the shape of the head and front legs of a galloping horse.

"Eek!" Pippa squealed.

Two giant seahorses popped through

the water and examined Pippa with their big eyes.

"You *are* real!" she exclaimed. "I knew I hadn't imagined it."

Pippa waded closer to the giant creatures and gently stroked their noses.

"Your name, Pippa, is short for Philippa, which means *lover of ponies*," said the pink seahorse.

"That's right," said Pippa, who couldn't believe she was talking to a giant seahorse.

"Then you are the one," said the green seahorse.

"My name is Rosella," the pink seahorse continued. "And this is Triton. We've come to take you to a place that needs your help."

With a flick of her pink tail, Rosella scooped Pippa up, placing her gently on her back. Then both seahorses surged forward through the foamy water.

"Where are we going?" Pippa asked.

"To Chevalia!"

Chapter 2

Pippa could not believe that she was riding a giant seahorse far out to sea. Rosella swam on, diving in and out of the waves, as Pippa clung to her gracefully arched neck. In a strange way, it was like riding a pony. Pippa stared at the delicate ears and long spines sticking out from the animal's neck.

Triton, the great green seahorse, was swimming next to her.

"Are you comfortable?" he asked kindly.

His voice was soft and deep, and it stopped Pippa from feeling scared. For a moment she was too speechless to answer.

"Yes, thank you," she whispered at last. "Are you taking me back to my mom? She'll be worrying like crazy."

Both seahorses chuckled.

"We're taking you somewhere very special, where time exists in a bubble," explained Rosella in a gentle voice. "You can stay there as long as you like and you won't be missed, for time will not pass in your own world."

"Where is it?" asked Pippa, her voice shaking with excitement.

"The island of Chevalia," said the seahorses.

Pippa looked out to the horizon and saw a large island surrounded by a long sandy beach.

"Wow!"

Pippa stared at the island in amazement. It was the most beautiful place she'd ever seen. So many questions were bubbling inside her, but before she could ask anything more, Rosella tipped her into the water and nudged her gently ashore.

"Chevalia is in danger, but you can help save it," said Rosella.

"Me? But how?"

"That is your quest," said Triton.

"Good luck, Pippa, lover of ponies," called Rosella.

She dived under the water with Triton and they swam away.

Pippa scrambled to her feet. She was standing on a sandy beach by the edge of a forest. At first it was very quiet. The only sound was the soft hiss of the waves gently lapping the shore.

Suddenly she heard a low drumming. Squinting into the sun, she saw a pony galloping toward her along the beach. Its long tail streamed out like a banner, and golden sand sprayed up from its hooves. Pippa's heart was racing. Who was this coming to meet her?

With a snort of surprise, the pony pulled up, sliding to a stop a few feet from Pippa. It was pure white and wore a tiara covered in sparkling pink diamonds. The pony's dark-brown eyes shone with excitement.

"A girl!" Reaching out, the pony touched Pippa with a velvety nose. "A real live girl!"

Pippa stared back.

"Y-you . . . you can talk?" she

stuttered. Pippa couldn't take her eyes off her. She was the most beautiful pony she'd ever seen.

"Of course," said the pony, tossing her head. "All ponies can talk, but only special humans can hear us. I'm Princess Stardust, seventh foal of the queen and king of Chevalia. What's your name?"

"Pippa," she answered. "I'm the . . . second child . . . of the MacDonald family . . . of Burlington Terrace."

"Have you been sent to help us?" Stardust's voice trembled.

"Help you?" repeated Pippa.

"To find the missing horseshoes," said Stardust impatiently. "If the eight magical horseshoes aren't found and returned to the Whispering Wall by sundown on Midsummer Day, then Chevalia will be lost forever. Quick! Jump on my back. I'll take you to the castle to meet my mother and father."

Excitement and fear fizzled through Pippa. She was on a secret island with talking ponies and she was going to meet the queen and king! She'd only ridden a few times—and never bare-back. But here in Chevalia, anything seemed possible. Pushing aside her fears, she jumped onto Stardust's back.

"Hold on to my mane!" called Stardust.

As Pippa sank her hands into Star-dust's silky mane, the pony spun around

and galloped across the beach toward the trees.

"We'll cut through the Wild Forest," Stardust neighed. "It's off limits, but it's the quickest way home."

Pippa could see eight tall towers rising above the treetops. The towers disappeared as Stardust entered the Wild Forest. Pippa shivered as the dark woods swallowed them too.

Chapter 3

There were lots of ponies in the forest, all with tangled manes and dirty coats. They were playing chasing games and having so much fun Pippa almost wished that there was time to stop and meet them. But Stardust thundered on, dodging bramble bushes and jumping over fallen trees. Pippa sat firmly, gripping with her knees and ducking to avoid the low-hanging branches. The

Wild Forest was on the side of a hill and as it grew steeper, Stardust slowed. She was breathing noisily and her sides were heaving.

"Stardust, stop and let me walk," Pippa called out.

"It's too dangerous for you," panted Stardust. "The forest is filled with quicksand that would swallow you whole."

Pippa gulped. She didn't like the idea of being eaten by sand.

"But don't worry," added Stardust. "I know the way!"

A little while later, the woods began to thin. Stardust sped up as they broke through the trees and came out on the edge of a large field. On the opposite side of the Wild Forest was a range of hills. To the right, at the other end of the field, Pippa saw a wide road, a collection of buildings, and a riding ring, where a group of ponies was gathered. Stardust started to gallop across the field toward the hills, when one of the ponies, waddling on stubby legs, noticed her.

"Princess Stardust! Come here at once!" she bellowed.

Stardust pretended not to hear, until the pony broke away from the group and galloped after them.

"Oh, horseflies!" Stardust exclaimed, pulling up and waiting.

"Who is it?" Pippa asked curiously, as the stocky brown pony hurried toward them.

Stardust rolled her eyes. "Mrs. Steeplechase, our nanny. She's just taken my brothers and sisters to school. I should be there too."

Mrs. Steeplechase stopped in front of Stardust, her nostrils flaring angrily.

"What do you think you are doing? The Wild Forest is *strictly* off limits."

"Sorry," Stardust apologized. "I thought school had been canceled because of the emergency. I was looking for the missing horseshoes, but instead I found Pippa. She's been sent to help us. Isn't that fantastic?"

Suddenly Mrs. Steeplechase noticed Pippa.

"A human girl!" she snorted with alarm. "And what's she doing riding on your back as if you were just any old pony? Get down, girl. You can walk the rest of the way."

"But—" said Stardust.

"Don't argue," said Mrs. Steeple-chase fiercely. "She might be dangerous. What will Queen Moonshine and King Firestar say about this? A girl indeed!"

Pippa's heart sank. She hoped that the king and queen weren't as unfriendly as the royal nanny. She turned pink with embarrassment and slid down from Stardust's back.

"Don't mind Mrs. Steeplechase— she's all whinny and no kick. Mom and Dad will be thrilled to see you," Stardust whispered. She began to mimic Mrs. Steeplechase, walking stiffly after her, copying the way Mrs. Steeple- chase's large bottom swung from side to side.

Giggling quietly, Pippa followed Stardust over the field and along a winding path. After a while, the path opened out at the top of a hill. Pippa stopped and stared.

Ahead of her, between the other hills, was Stableside Castle, the biggest castle she'd ever seen. Its white stone walls sparkled like pearls in the bright sunlight. Eight flags, each a different color but all decorated with a golden horseshoe, fluttered from the tall towers, and the enormous wooden drawbridge was lowered, as if to welcome them.

"That's my tower," Stardust said, pointing her nose at the smallest one, which was topped by a pink flag, waving in the breeze. "It's got the best view in the whole castle."

A group of horses was standing by the drawbridge with cameras around their necks, obviously waiting for someone to come or go.

Mrs. Steeplechase shook her head. "The ponarazzi are still here then! We'll have to take the secret path and go in through the back way, or else the girl's picture will be all over the island by tomorrow."

"They're always trying to take pictures of the Royal Family," said Stardust.

"No talking and hurry up," Mrs. Steeplechase said sternly, as she trotted down the hill toward a small door hidden in the castle's walls.

Pippa felt butterflies in her stomach as she followed behind Mrs. Steeplechase. Stardust's hooves crunched on the white gravel at the base of the castle wall, and Mrs. Steeplechase turned to Stardust.

"Try to trot quietly, child," she said.

But Stardust ignored her nanny and continued to clatter beside her. She did not seem worried that she was in trouble.

The hidden door led into a large courtyard with a stage on one side, and a huge stone wall behind it. The wall was bare except for eight imprints of horseshoes. Stardust blinked back a tear.

"That's where the golden horseshoes should hang," she whispered.

A wave of sadness hit Pippa and she had to catch her breath. She glanced around and saw piles of silk ribbons and flowers on the ground. It was as if the courtyard had been abandoned suddenly. A small chestnut pony was sweeping them up. A trail of black hoof-prints led to the door they'd come in. Pippa stared at the hoofprints. Something about them bothered her, but she couldn't quite put her finger on it.

"We were decorating the castle for the Midsummer Ball," Stardust said, nodding at the ribbons. "But now no one has the heart to get things ready. It's only a week away and it takes forever to prepare everything, especially the food for the banquet."

Mrs. Steeplechase trotted across the courtyard to a wooden door guarded by a black pony wearing a red sash. The pony bowed his head, then nudged open the door.

"This is the Royal Court," Stardust

whispered, as they entered a large room full of perfectly groomed ponies with gleaming coats and polished hooves.

One by one they fell silent, staring at Pippa with wide eyes as she walked across the room. Pippa felt very small as she made her way nervously through the crowd. All the ponies wore brightly

colored sashes, some decorated with jewels. A chestnut pony with big eyes, a square nose, and emeralds in her mane gave Pippa a very mean look. Next to her, a smaller pony with the same shaped nose and eyes gave her an identical hard stare.

"That's Baroness Divine and her daughter Cinders," whispered Stardust. "No one likes them. They think they're so much better than anyone else. Cinders shouldn't even be here. She should be at school, like me."

Mrs. Steeplechase stopped in front of a beautiful palomino pony with a long white mane and tail, and a large copper-colored pony. Stiffly, she bent one leg, bowing her head to the ground. Stardust copied, leaving Pippa standing awkwardly between them. Unsure what to do, Pippa curtsied as if she was greeting her ballet teacher.

"Your Majesties," said Mrs. Steeplechase, rising slowly. "Princess Stardust has found a stranger on our island. A human."

"So I can see," said the queen, her brown eyes resting on Pippa. "What is your name, child? And where do you come from?"

Suddenly Pippa felt very shy. She stuttered her name.

"P-P-Pippa MacDonald. From Burlington Terrace."

"Isn't it wonderful!" said Stardust. "Pippa's been sent to help us find the missing horseshoes."

All the ponies in the room began

to whisper. Baroness Divine stepped forward.

"No human has ever set foot on Chevalia before. How can we trust her?" she demanded.

"She's a pony lover," said Stardust angrily. "Only a true pony lover can find Chevalia and understand our language."

Queen Moonshine stared at Pippa, making her squirm inside, but she stood tall, hoping the queen would see that she had nothing to hide.

"Chevalia is a very special place. It needs horse and pony lovers from around the world to keep it alive," the queen said in a low voice. "Their love is captured by the eight magical horse-shoes that hang on the Whispering

Wall. Once a year, the magic in those horseshoes must be renewed by the Midsummer sun or it will fade. If that happens, then our beautiful island will sink into the sea."

Pippa gulped. Now she understood why Princess Stardust was so sad that the wall was bare.

"This is a time of great danger," Baroness Divine said. "Midsummer Day will be here soon but the magical horse-shoes have disappeared. How did you get here? Who told you that Chevalia needed help? How do we know we can trust you?"

Chapter 4

The Royal Court was so quiet that Pippa was sure everyone would hear her heart thudding.

"I didn't know Chevalia needed my help," she answered truthfully. "I was on vacation with my family when a magic wave scooped me up. Rosella and Triton brought me here."

The ponies stared at Pippa in awe. An excited murmur rippled around the regal room.

"The human girl saw Rosella and Triton—but why? They never show themselves to humans," a pony said.

The queen stamped a hoof for silence.

"There is an old legend that tells of a human girl who comes to Chevalia in its time of need. The seahorses brought you here, so I believe you are that girl." She touched Pippa on the top of her head with her muzzle. "Welcome to Chevalia. Good luck with your quest. If there is anything you need, then please ask."

"She needs me," Stardust said, trotting forward.

Mrs. Steeplechase frowned.

"Hush," she scolded. "You may only speak to the queen when she speaks to you."

"But Pippa is *my* pet! I found her. Besides, how else will she find her way around the island?" Stardust insisted.

The queen tried not to smile.

"I'm sure we can find Pippa a good guide," she answered. "Perhaps your big sister Crystal—"

"I'd really like Stardust to help me," Pippa said bravely, interrupting the queen.

The queen looked uncertain.

"Let Stardust help," the king said. "It will be good for her to have some responsibility for a change."

"Very well," said the queen. "You'd better start right away. Time is running out."

"Thanks, Mom," whinnied Stardust.

"Your Majesty," she added quickly, when Mrs. Steeplechase glared at her.

As Stardust and Pippa left the court, Cinders started complaining.

"It's not fair," she whispered loudly, so that Pippa could hear. "Princess Stardust gets everything. I want a girl too. I've wanted one much longer than she has."

"Hush," said the baroness. "Better things come to those who wait."

"What does she mean?" asked Pippa.

"Don't pay any attention to her—she's always been jealous of the Royal Family," said Stardust. "Come on. Let's start searching for the missing horseshoes."

Stardust used the same hidden door they'd entered the castle by.

"Where are we going first?" asked Pippa.

"Mane Street," said Stardust. "It's where everyone hangs out."

"It doesn't sound like a very good hiding place," Pippa said doubtfully.

"Exactly!" said Stardust. "If I were hiding something, that's where I'd put it, because no one would think to look there. Hop on my back. It's so much fun when we gallop together."

"But what about Mrs. Steeplechase?" asked Pippa.

"Horseflies to Mrs. Steeplechase! Mom and Dad didn't tell you not to ride me, did they?"

Pippa didn't need a second invitation. She loved riding Stardust, and her mouth stretched into a wide grin as she jumped onto her back.

☆

Mane Street was the wide, grassy road on the field that they had crossed earlier.

"That's my school," Stardust said proudly, as they passed Canter's Prep School for Fine Equine. "Miss Huckleby is the best teacher ever. You should hear her read *Black Beauty*."

Stardust's school was a blue wooden building with window boxes overflowing with colorful flowers and tubs filled with carrot sprouts.

"The carrots are for snacking on," Stardust said, pulling up two and giving one to Pippa.

Crunching on their carrots, they

peered in through the windows, where a class of ponies was starting a math lesson.

Stardust giggled.

"Look at Honey admiring her sparkly hoof polish. She's my third-oldest sister. The grumpy-looking pony wearing the boring wooden tiara with the acorns is Cloud, my second-oldest sister. My

oldest sister is Crystal. She's left Canter's now. She's going to be queen one day, and she never lets us forget it!"

Cloud turned to the window with a scowl, and Stardust quickly pulled Pippa away.

"Don't let her see you," she said. "She'd want to know why I'm not in school, and there isn't time to explain."

They crept around the back of the school, passing the riding ring Pippa had seen earlier, and a green field where some tiny ponies were learning to trot. Stardust barely glanced their way, but Pippa held back, sure she saw something shining in the long grass at the edge of the field. Could it be one of the missing golden horseshoes? She hurried over and was disappointed to find it was just an ordinary old horseshoe.

Pippa's eyes grew wider and wider as Stardust pranced along Mane Street pointing out all her favorite stores. Pippa noticed that all the shoppers were staring back at her too!

"That's the salon where I go to have my mane and tail washed. They have gorgeous strawberry-scented shampoo. And look—Dolly's Tea Rooms. You should taste their buckets of hot carrot juice. Delicious!" Stardust said, smacking her lips. "And there's Mr. Gem's. He sells the nicest jewels ever."

It reminded Pippa of the main street back at home, only Mane Street was much prettier, with beds of sunflowers decorating the sidewalks and tiny silver horseshoes strung from the old-fashioned streetlights. Everything was spotlessly clean—even the silver water troughs had been polished until they shone. The street was packed with ponies, and Pippa was amazed to see so many different types. There were well-groomed ponies, stocky working ones, and scruffy little Shetlands. Everyone seemed very quiet, mostly talking in whispers. When a pony whinnied with laughter, the others frowned.

"It's been like this since the horse-shoes went missing," sighed Stardust.

Pippa was beginning to doubt that they'd find any of the golden horseshoes here. There were too many ponies and

not enough hiding places. There was an amusement park at the end of the street, though. That looked like a more promising place to hide things.

"Should we look in there?" she asked.

"That's where I'm taking you!" Stardust said excitedly. "You should see the merry-go-round. It's rainbow-colored with tiny flashing lights. It's so pretty. And the ghost train is really scary. It's even got Night Mares."

"Night Mares?" asked Pippa. "What do you mean?"

"The Night Mares are spooky-looking ponies. They've lived here forever, even when Chevalia was just a tiny lump of volcanic rock and not the magical island it is today. I've never seen one, but

everyone says they're really mean." Stardust shivered. "Do you want a ride on the ghost train? It's a lot of fun."

"I thought we were looking for the horseshoes," said Pippa.

Stardust blushed.

"We are! It's just so wonderful having you here, and I want to show you everything. But you're right. Finding the horseshoes is the most important thing. Without them Chevalia will lose its magic."

Stardust shuddered, her brown eyes suddenly glistening with tears.

"Don't worry," Pippa said, stroking her neck. "I promise we'll find the horseshoes."

"Really?" Stardust sniffed. "Thank you, Pippa. You're the best pet ever."

Pippa opened her mouth to argue that she wasn't a pet, but Stardust was already heading into the amusement park.

The amusement park was less crowded than Mane Street. None of the ponies, except for the really young ones, seemed to be enjoying themselves.

Pippa and Stardust walked around the rides but found nothing.

"Let's search the rest of the fields," Stardust said finally. "They're big enough to hide all eight of the horseshoes."

☆

Pippa and Stardust spent the rest of the day walking the fields. It was hard work and there were many false alarms. By late afternoon Pippa had met many of Stardust's friends, and they had both found lots of precious items that other young ponies had lost—like hair clips and combs—but they hadn't found any of the golden horseshoes.

As the sun began to set, they made their way back to the castle. Pippa was hungry and very frustrated that they

hadn't discovered any clues about where the missing horseshoes might be.

"We both need a hoof massage with dandelion hoof balm," Stardust said longingly, as they passed the Mane Street Salon. "But Mrs. Steeplechase is very strict about mealtimes. She won't let us go out together tomorrow if we're late."

"We *must* find those magical horse-shoes tomorrow," said Pippa.

☆

Meals were eaten in a huge dining room with three stone feeding troughs, and a special gold one at the front of the room for the queen and king. Everyone stared at Pippa as she followed Stardust to a trough.

As the serving ponies carried in buckets of steaming oats and mashed carrots, Pippa wondered what she was going to eat, but she didn't need to worry. One of the cooks came out of the kitchen to serve her personally.

"Chicken fingers and fries!" Pippa cried delightedly. "My favorite!"

There was even a knife and fork to

eat with. As Pippa began to eat, Stardust watched in amazement.

"So that's what those are for!" she exclaimed. "I've only ever seen them in the Museum of Human Artifacts."

Pippa laughed, and listened to the ponies whinnying around her. Most of their chatter was about the missing horseshoes. Pippa caught her own name several times and a few of the ponies shyly nodded at her. But not everyone was as friendly. Several refused to look, turning away if Pippa smiled at them. She finished her meal with a rosy red apple. It felt good to eat after such a busy day.

When Stardust and Pippa left the dining room to go to bed, one pony neighed at them as they passed.

"It's funny how the girl arrived at the same time that the horseshoes disappeared. I don't trust her."

The words stung, but Pippa held her head up high. The ponies of Chevalia needed her, and she wasn't going to let them down.

Chapter 5

Stardust's room was right at the top of the eighth tower of the castle. Instead of stairs, there was a spiral ramp. It was large and round, with curved stone walls. On her dressing table, in a special place, was a little doll that had washed up on shore.

"I've wanted a girl ever since I was a foal, but I never dreamed I'd get one," Stardust explained.

"I've wanted a pony forever too," said Pippa.

Stardust looked confused but then she laughed.

"I get it! You're my pet and I'm yours."

"Can't we just be friends?" Pippa asked.

"Friends," Stardust said slowly. "That sounds nice. Yes, let's be friends."

"You're a magical friend," said Pippa.

"No, you're a magical friend." Stardust laughed again.

Stardust slept in a huge bed with a straw blanket and a horseshoe-shaped headboard covered with ribbons. Pippa slept on a special cot next to her. The bed was surprisingly comfortable, and she fell asleep immediately.

☆

The next morning, Pippa woke up early. Stardust was still snoring softly, so she stared out of the window. Pippa was terrified of heights and at first it made her feel sick being so high up. Taking deep breaths, she looked out over the magical island. It calmed her to think about all these ponies living together in such a special place. She watched the ponies strolling on Mane Street, and in the distance she spotted ponies working in the fields. As she looked out to the sea, she could see nothing around for miles, and she reminded herself that Chevalia would be lost if she didn't keep her promise.

Pippa counted the days on her

fingers. There were only six left until Midsummer. Time was running out. They had to find the golden horseshoes before it was too late. Yesterday had been fun, but Pippa worried that Stardust had been more excited about touring Chevalia and showing off her new friend than she had been about searching for the missing horseshoes. Today would be different. Pippa decided it was time to take charge.

Anxious to get started, Pippa gently shook the pony awake.

"You're still here!" Stardust whinnied with delight as she opened her eyes. "I thought I might have dreamed you."

Quickly, she rolled out of bed and nuzzled Pippa's dark hair.

"Me too," said Pippa. "But it's not a dream, and we're going to find the missing horseshoes."

Stardust took a long time getting ready so Pippa helped, combing her mane and tail, to hurry her along.

"I've been wondering where to go today," Stardust said. "We could visit the Grasslands or the beaches. Or perhaps we should start with the Savannah, where the striped ponies roam wild. Then there's the Horseshoe Hills and the Volcano. Maybe not the Volcano—it's spooky there." Stardust shivered.

Pippa stopped combing as an idea clicked into place.

"The Volcano!" she exclaimed. "Maybe that would explain the black

hoof marks I saw in the courtyard yesterday. I wondered where they'd come from. Everywhere in Chevalia seems so clean, especially around the castle, but volcanoes are covered in ash."

"Are you sure?" Stardust asked uncertainly. "Wouldn't you rather search the beaches? We might find some clues there."

"But the black hoof marks are a clue!" Pippa said, her voice rising with excitement. "We *have* to search the Volcano."

"I'm not sure," Stardust said reluctantly. "Storm—he's my youngest brother—told me never to go there. It's too dangerous."

"Then I'll go on my own," Pippa said stubbornly.

Stardust's eyes widened.

"You'd really do that?"

Pippa nodded. She'd promised to save Chevalia and she would keep her word, no matter how dangerous it was.

"Then I'm coming with you," said Stardust.

Pippa hugged Stardust around the neck, pleased that she didn't have to go to the Volcano alone.

Even though she was nervous, Pippa was impatient to get started. After a quick breakfast of cereal and apples, she and Stardust went to the back door. It was very early and the door was still locked. Stardust pulled back the bolts with her teeth.

"Maybe the Night Mares stole our horseshoes," said Stardust. "Storm thinks that they live on the Volcano, but Comet, my bookworm brother, says that's just a myth. But if it was the Night Mares, then how did they get inside the castle? All the doors are locked from the inside at night."

"Maybe someone helped them," suggested Pippa.

"No!" Stardust exclaimed, sounding shocked. "Why would anyone do that?"

Pippa shrugged. She didn't know either. Chevalia was so special, she couldn't imagine anyone wanting to harm it.

Pippa could hardly believe how much her riding had improved in such a short time. She felt as comfortable riding Stardust bareback as if she'd been riding with a saddle. How impressed her pony-crazy friends back home would be if they could see her now!

At last, they entered the foothills,

staying on the path so that they didn't get lost. The higher they went, the steeper the path grew. Sometimes it ran alongside the cliff. Pippa didn't like that—it made her dizzy to look down and see the jagged rocks falling away beneath her. Stardust seemed to sense her fear and kept away from the edge.

It was very peaceful. The only sounds were the clopping of Stardust's hooves, the cry of the birds soaring overhead, and a soft rushing noise that Pippa couldn't figure out until they reached a small stream that crossed the path.

"So that's what I could hear," Pippa said, as Stardust jumped the stream then stopped for a drink.

"Try some," she said. "It's fresh and it's clean."

76

Pippa slid from Stardust's back and, kneeling down, scooped up the water in cupped hands. It was freezing cold and made her fingers tingle.

"Mmm, that's delicious," she said, enjoying a long drink.

Stardust nudged her playfully, her long white mane falling over Pippa's arm.

"That tickles!" Pippa giggled, nudging Stardust back.

Stardust dipped a hoof in the stream, splashing water at Pippa.

"Water fight!" she neighed.

"Water fight!" Pippa agreed, splashing Stardust back.

Stardust splashed with her hooves and Pippa with her feet. They both disappeared in a shower of water, which

sparkled like diamonds in the sunshine, until Pippa and Stardust were soaking wet.

"Stop!" Pippa begged, laughing, pushing her soggy curls away from her face.

"That was so much fun," Stardust whinnied, shaking herself dry and soaking Pippa all over again.

"Eeww!" squealed Pippa. "I didn't think I could get any wetter!"

It was already very hot, and as the friends climbed higher the sun soon dried Pippa's clothes. After a while, they followed another stream that snaked alongside the path before tumbling over a cliff in a fast-flowing waterfall.

"It's beautiful!" Pippa gasped.

"Chevalia is beautiful," Stardust said, her face clouding with worry. "I can't understand why the Night Mares would want to harm it."

"It might not have been them," said Pippa.

"Who else could it have been?" Stardust asked. "No one knows about

Chevalia. Only true pony lovers can see it, and a true pony lover would never harm us."

Pippa twisted a curl of her hair around her finger. "But the island's not going to disappear. We're going to find the golden horseshoes."

"Promise?" asked Stardust.

"Yes," said Pippa.

Knowing it was a sign of friendship in ponies, she leaned forward, softly blowing air at Stardust's nostrils.

Stardust blew air back.

"Thank you, Pippa," she whispered. "You're a true friend."

Pippa pushed away her worries as she smiled at Stardust. Promises were easy to make, but could she really keep hers?

Yes, she told herself firmly. She would not break her word. She *would* find the golden horseshoes in time to save Chevalia.

Chapter 6

As Pippa and Stardust neared the bottom of the Volcano, the path grew steeper. It was covered with black rocks.

"They're hot!" exclaimed Pippa. She picked one up and quickly put it down again, brushing the black dirt from her hands.

"Yes, and this is as far as we can go," Stardust said nervously. "I think the Night Mares live near here."

"So now we look for clues?" Pippa asked.

Stardust nodded.

"But only on this side of the Volcano. We can't stray into the Cloud Forest on the other side. No one's allowed to go there. Not even Mom and Dad."

"Why not?" asked Pippa.

"It's haunted," she whispered.

"Oh," Pippa said, feeling both scared and relieved.

The Volcano was so big it would have taken forever if they'd had to search it all. She hoped she wouldn't have to look for the horseshoes in a haunted forest.

Side by side, Pippa and Stardust started to hunt for clues. At first

Pippa was very excited, thinking that they might find all eight of the horseshoes. The rocky landscape had lots of nooks and crannies, perfect for hiding things in. Each time she saw something shining in the sun Pippa rushed forward, and each time she was disappointed.

"I'm thirsty," Stardust said at last. Her white coat was smudged with dirt and her long tail was full of tangles. "Let's go back to the stream for a drink."

She was trotting toward the path when something soared overhead.

"What's that?" Pippa cried, pointing upward.

Stardust swung around.

"What?" she asked. "I can't see anything."

"It's gone." Pippa was dismayed.

"Maybe it was an eagle?" said Stardust.

Pippa fell silent. The thing she'd seen had been far too big to be an eagle. As she followed Stardust to the stream, the creature flew over again. Pippa's eyes widened.

"Look!" she shouted. "It's a flying horse!"

Stardust spun around again.

"Peggy!" she exclaimed.

Peggy had a silvery coat, a long mane and tail, and an enormous pair of feathery wings. She circled overhead, tilting slightly as she drifted through the air.

"She's amazing," Pippa breathed, her heart thudding. "Stardust, I think she's trying to tell us something!"

"I don't think so," said Stardust. "Peggy hardly ever shows herself— you're lucky to have seen her. I think she's curious about you."

Pippa shielded her eyes with her hands as she squinted at the flying horse.

"But look how she keeps dipping her wing. It's at the same place every time. And then she turns her head to see if we're watching her."

Stardust stared in silence.

"It might be nothing, but maybe we should check it out," she said at last.

Forgetting their thirst, Pippa and

Stardust hurried back the way they'd come. Peggy remained overhead, still flying in the same circle, until the friends were directly underneath her. Suddenly she swooped much lower, hovering right above a rocky ledge. Whinnying loudly, she reared up. Then, with a flick of her silvery tail, she flew away.

"Look!" Pippa said, breaking into a run. "There's something sparkly up there on the ledge."

Pippa and Stardust raced across the rocks until they reached the ledge that Peggy had shown them.

Stardust neighed with excitement.

"I can see something shining in the grass."

Pippa stood on tiptoe. In the middle of a clump of grass, something was shining with a soft yellow glow.

"It must be one of our golden horseshoes!" she exclaimed.

The horseshoe was so well hidden that if it hadn't been for Peggy, Pippa and Stardust would never have spotted it. Nervously, Pippa rubbed her hands on her shorts. The ledge was more than twice her height and she'd have to climb it to reach the horseshoe. The thought made her feel hot and shaky. She couldn't do it. The ledge was much too high.

"Stand on my back," Stardust said eagerly.

Pippa had always been afraid of heights. She didn't move.

"Don't worry—you won't hurt me. I'm really strong," Stardust said, misunderstanding Pippa's reaction.

Pippa was still a little scared, but she jumped onto Stardust's back. She sat for a moment to work up the courage to keep going.

Come on, you can do this, she silently urged herself.

Slowly, Pippa stood up. Her heart was racing and her legs shook like a jellyfish. Stardust remained completely still, and slowly Pippa relaxed. That wasn't so bad! Now all she had to do was stretch up to grab the missing horseshoe. But frustratingly, it was just out of reach. Pippa stretched as far as she dared—any farther and she'd lose her balance.

"It's no good," she called at last. "I can't get it. Can you move any closer?"

"I'm as close as I can get," said Stardust.

Pippa stared at the ground and immediately wished she hadn't. Quickly, she sat back down, clinging on to

Stardust's mane until her head stopped swimming.

"Are you okay?" asked Stardust.

"I'm fine," Pippa replied, licking her dry lips.

She was going to have to dismount and climb up to the ledge instead. But as she slid down from Stardust's back, she saw a long, sturdy stick. Snatching it up, she waved it in relief.

"I might be able to reach the horse-shoe with this."

Being careful not to hit Stardust with the stick, Pippa scrambled onto her back once more. But as she reached up to hook the horseshoe, she froze. What was that? Above the ledge, to the right, was a large slab of rock, where two scruffy-looking ponies with thin, straggly manes and tails were arguing loudly. Pippa's insides turned to ice.

"They must be Night Mares!" she whispered.

Chapter 7

Pippa stayed still and listened to the Night Mares' argument.

"How did you manage to drop a horseshoe, Nightshade?" the smaller pony whinnied angrily. "The Mistress said to hide it carefully so that the Royal Ponies wouldn't find it! It just goes to show that even though you're bigger than me, you're not smarter."

"Be quiet, Eclipse. Nagging me isn't

94

going to help me get the horseshoe back," Nightshade whinnied.

"But how will we reach it from here?"

"Use that branch behind you."

As Eclipse turned to look at the branch, Pippa snapped into action. With trembling hands, she reached up to hook the golden horseshoe down from the ledge. It was very heavy, and although Pippa's stick was long enough to touch it, she couldn't drag the horseshoe toward her. Swallowing her frustration, she tried again.

"What's happening?" called Stardust. "Have you got it yet?"

"Shhh," whispered Pippa.

But it was too late.

"Who's that?" asked Nightshade. She

peered over the rock and her eyes
locked with Pippa's. "Eclipse, it's a
girl!" she neighed. "And she's stealing
my horseshoe!"

"Prancing ponies!" cursed Eclipse.

Breathing heavily, Pippa blocked
out Nightshade and Eclipse's frantic

conversation and concentrated on getting the horseshoe. Using both hands to hold the stick, and hoping that Stardust wouldn't move a muscle, she dragged the horseshoe down. But Eclipse had also found a stick on the ground, and she was trying to pull the horseshoe up. It was turning into a tug of war! Eclipse's stick was larger than Pippa's, but the pony was holding it in her mouth and having trouble controlling it. Steadily, Pippa dragged the horseshoe to the edge of the ledge. As she reached out to pick it up, Eclipse brought her stick crashing down.

Just in time, Pippa snatched her hand out of the way. She sat down on

Stardust's back and tightly clutched the horseshoe.

"I've got it!" she said triumphantly.

"Hold on tight!" Stardust said, turning sharply to gallop back down the Volcano.

"That's *my* horseshoe!" Nightshade shouted after her.

As Stardust gathered speed, her hooves thumping on the ash-covered path, the Night Mares' voices faded away.

Pippa started to wonder who Eclipse had meant by "the Mistress." She clung on to Stardust, wrapping her free hand around the white mane and gripping with her knees. Stardust didn't stop until she was safely at the bottom of the Volcano, where she pulled up in the shade of a tree. Pippa slid down from her back and fanned her friend with a feathery green leaf. It was several minutes before Stardust caught her breath.

"We did it," Stardust said, trembling with excitement. "We found our first

horseshoe. I can't wait to show Mom and Dad. They'll be thrilled!"

Pippa's smile was so wide it almost reached her ears, but her stomach felt nervous. That had been so scary.

"So you were right—it *was* the Night Mares who stole the horseshoes!"

She hoped the other seven horse-shoes would be easier to retrieve, but what if they couldn't find them?

"What do you think?" Stardust asked impatiently, pawing the ground with a hoof.

"Sorry, what did you say?" Pippa realized that she hadn't been listening.

"Nightshade and Eclipse think we've gone home," Stardust repeated. "We could sneak back and follow them.

They might say where the other horse-shoes are—or who this mysterious Mistress is."

Pippa slid the golden horseshoe into her pocket.

"I think we should take this one back to the castle first and hang it where it belongs. We don't want to lose it again."

Stardust sighed. Her new friend was very sensible.

"You're right. The horseshoe needs to be back on the wall so that it can pick up the love from all the horse and pony lovers around the world. It's what keeps Chevalia alive."

In silence, they hurried to the castle, entering by the back door and going straight to the Royal Court.

As the guard opened the large wooden door, Pippa pulled the horseshoe from her pocket and handed it to Stardust.

"You take this," she said.

"No way!" exclaimed Stardust. "You rescued it. You can give it to Mom and Dad."

The Royal Court was packed and noisy, but when the ponies saw the golden horseshoe they immediately fell silent. Pippa followed Stardust over to her parents.

Queen Moonshine's eyes lit up with joy.

"You've found one of our horseshoes!" she whinnied. "That's wonderful. I'm so proud of you both."

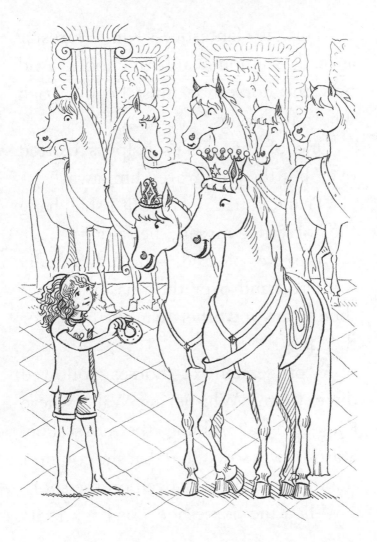

"This is fantastic," King Firestar agreed, stamping a large hoof. "And now the horseshoe must be put back where it belongs."

One of the court's helpers trotted over, but the king waved him away.

"Thank you, Conker, but I shall hang the horseshoe myself," he said.

Pippa was pleased—she didn't really want to hand over the missing horse-shoe to anyone other than the queen or the king.

A procession of horses followed them to the Whispering Wall, where King Firestar rehung the horseshoe. Stardust was so excited that she couldn't stand still, and she danced on the spot.

When the horseshoe was back in its

place, the crowd neighed loudly. But the single horseshoe looked very small and lonely hanging on the wall.

Pippa clapped, but part of her felt worried. There was still so much to do.

"Congratulations," Queen Moonshine said in a low voice. "But your quest has only just begun. Midsummer Day will soon be here and there are still seven horseshoes to find. Go safely, my children, and remember not to count your horseshoes until they're hung!"

"We won't, Your Majesty," Pippa said earnestly.

Both the queen's words and seeing the golden horseshoe hanging on the wall had filled her with a new confidence. They could do this. Together she and Stardust would find all the missing horseshoes.

"To Chevalia!" she cheered.

"To Chevalia!" Stardust echoed. "And to you, Pippa, my magical friend!"

Will Pippa and Princess Stardust
find all the golden horseshoes?

DON'T MISS THEIR NEXT ADVENTURE
AT THE EQUESTRIATHON!

Turn the page to read a sneak peek . . .

"Ponies and foals, please show your appreciation for the arrival of Their Majesties Queen Moonshine, King Firestar, and the Prince and Princess Ponies: Crystal, Jet, Cloud, Honey, Comet, Storm, and—not forgetting the little foal of the family—Stardust. Plus our very special guest, Pippa MacDonald."

There was a thunderous roar and the ground shook with even more stamping. Pippa's face felt hot and her chest tightened as she stared shyly at the enormous crowd. She'd never seen so many ponies all in one place. There was every kind, from tiny Shetlands with shaggy manes covering their eyes to magnificent thoroughbreds with highly polished coats.

"Mmm, can you smell that carrot juice?" said Stardust. "I could drink a whole trough of it."

"You're only hungry because you slept through breakfast," Cloud said irritably.

"I could drink a troughful of carrot juice too," said Honey. "Let's go and get some together. Do you like my hooves by the way? I wasn't sure which color to paint them."

"I *love* your hooves," said Stardust.

"They are pretty," Pippa said, taking in Honey's glittery pink-and-purple-striped hooves.

"Where did you get the polish from?" asked Stardust.

"The Mane Street Salon. Excuse me!" Honey said angrily, as Crystal and Jet pushed past to get to the front of the royal box.

"Out of my way, Jet. The crowds are here to see me," said Crystal.

"No, they're not," Jet said, winking at a group of young fillies and grinning when they blushed. "It's me they're here for."

"Well, they're certainly not here for me," Storm said, smiling at Pippa.

"I'm not surprised," Crystal said moodily. "You might have cleaned up your hooves at least, Storm, before coming to stand in the royal box."

"Don't worry, Storm," Stardust whispered. "No one's interested in me either."

Pippa sighed. Stardust seemed to have forgotten they had an important job to do.

"I'm going to start looking for the horseshoes," Pippa said impatiently.

"Wait for me! Sorry, Honey, I've got to go," added Stardust. She hurried after Pippa, stepping out of the royal box and into the crowd.

"We'll never find anything here. There are too many ponies around!" Pippa worried. Then she thought of something. "Do you think the crowd would help us?"

"That's a great idea!" said Stardust.

Stardust's excitement was contagious, and she soon had a group of eager ponies helping her to search the show ground. Pippa tried asking for their help too, but most of the ponies just stared at her in awe. They had never seen a real live girl before. In the end she gave up asking and searched alone, keeping her head down to avoid all the curious stares.

The dressage competition started and many of the ponies lost interest in searching for the horseshoes and trotted

over to the arena to watch. The Royal
Family was settled in the royal box,
enjoying the Games. Honey had a large
bag of roasted nuts that Stardust kept
looking at longingly.

"Let's go and watch the dressage for
a bit," she said at last, when she couldn't
resist any longer.

"We can't," said Pippa. "There are only five days left until Midsummer."

Stardust nuzzled her nose in Pippa's dark, wavy hair.

"I know," she said softly. "But you heard what Mom said about the Royal Ponies needing to act normally. Let's search for a bit longer and then we really have to go and watch some of the events."

Among the trees at the edge of the show ground was a temporary stable block for the competitors. It was packed with ponies combing their manes and painting their hooves. Sashes and tail bandages fluttered from the trees and there was a strong smell of hoof oil.

A flash of light caught Pippa's eye. It was coming from a hollow in a wizened old tree. Something shiny was hidden inside. Her heart quickened as she went toward the light and pulled out the shiny object.

"It's just a hoof pick," she said, her shoulders sagging with disappointment.

"That's my lucky hoof pick!" said an excited voice. "At least, I hope it's lucky."

Pippa turned around to see a solid, chestnut pony, with a neatly braided mane tied with blue ribbons, trotting up behind her.

"Blossom!" Stardust whinnied, blowing through her nostrils at the pony.

Blossom blew back, giggling as they touched noses.

"Are you competing in the junior dressage?" asked Stardust.

"I can't get out of it," Blossom said sadly. "You will come and watch me, won't you? Pleeeeease! I know I'll mess it all up if my best friend isn't there to cheer me on."

"I'll try," Stardust said. "But Pippa

and I are busy right now. Pippa's here to find the missing horseshoes and I'm helping her."

A hurt look crossed Blossom's face, but she swallowed and said bravely, "I know. Everyone's talking about her—a real live girl here on Chevalia."

"She's my best pet ever," Stardust said proudly.

Pippa rolled her eyes and cleared her throat, hoping that Stardust would remember that she wasn't a pet.

"I mean, Pippa's my best friend," Stardust said quickly, realizing her mistake.

Pippa noticed that Blossom's big brown eyes glittered with tears.

"B-b-best friend?" she stuttered. "I thought I was your best friend."

"You are. Well, you were until Pippa arrived," Stardust said. She did not see that Blossom was sad. "Pippa's my best friend now, but you can be my second best."

Just then the announcer called for the start of the junior dressage competition.

"Listen—they're calling your class," said Stardust. "You'd better go."

"So are you coming to watch me?"

"I'm sorry, Blossom, but Pippa and I—"

"We'd love to watch," Pippa interrupted. "We'll both cheer you on!"